# LADIES ALMANACK

NOW AS A WONDER WORKER, DAME MUSSET WAS PERHAPS AT HER VERY BEST WHEN, CARRYING A POLE AND SPORTING A MUFF, AND AN ENDEARING TIPPET, SHE STEPPED OUT UPON THAT EXCEEDING THIN ICE TO WHICH IT HAS PLEASED GOD, MORE AND MORE TO CALL FRAIL WOMAN,

THERE SO CONDUCTING HERSELF THAT NONE WERE PUT TO THE CHAGRIN OF SINKING FOR THE THIRD TIME!

# LADIES ALMANACK

*showing their Signs and their tides;
their Moons and their Changes;
the Seasons as it is with them;
their Eclipses and Equinoxes; as
well as a full Record of diurnal
and nocturnal Distempers*

WRITTEN & ILLUSTRATED

## BY A LADY OF FASHION

## DALKEY ARCHIVE PRESS

Originally published 1928
Afterword © 1992 by Dalkey Archive Press

Library of Congress Cataloging-in-Publication Data
Barnes, Djuna.
  Ladies almanack: showing their signs and their tides, their moons and their changes, the seasons as it is with them, their eclipses and equinoxes, as well as a full record of diurnal and nocturnal distempers / written & illustrated by a lady of fashion.
  I. Title.
PS3502.A614L3     1992
818'.5207—dc20     91-14515
ISBN: 0-916583-88-0

First printing: January 1992
Second printing: January 1995


Dalkey Archive Press
Campus Box 4241
Normal, IL 61790-4241


*Printed on permanent/durable acid-free paper and bound in the United States of America.*

THE COOK HER RECIPES

THE PRIEST BREVIARY

THE DOCTOR PHYSIC

THE LION HIS ROAR

THE BRIDE HER FEARS

LADIES ALMANACK

THE BOOK ALL LADIES SHOULD CARRY

# LADIES ALMANACK

Now this be a Tale of as fine a Wench as ever wet Bed, she who was called Evangeline Musset and who was in her Heart one Grand Red Cross for the Pursuance, the Relief and the Distraction, of such Girls as in their Hinder Parts, and their Fore Parts, and in whatsoever Parts did suffer them most, lament Cruelly, be it Itch of Palm, or Quarters most horribly burning, which do oft occur in the Spring of the Year, or at those Times when they do sit upon warm and cozy Material, such as Fur, or thick and Oriental Rugs, (whose very Design it seems, procures for them such a Languishing of the Haunch and Reins as is insupportable) or who sit upon warm Stoves, whence it is known that one such flew up with an " Ah my God ! What a World it is for a Girl indeed, be she ever so well abridged and cool of Mind and preserved of Intention, the Instincts are, nevertheless, brought to such a yelping Pitch and so undo her, that she runs hither and thither seeking some Simple or Unguent which shall allay her Pain ! And why is it no Philosopher of whatever Sort, has discovered, amid the nice Herbage of his Garden, one that will content that Part, but that from the day that we were indifferent Matter, to this wherein we are Imperial Personages of the divine human Race, no thing so solaces it as other Parts as inflamed, or with the Consolation every Woman has at her Finger Tips, or at the very Hang of her Tongue ?"

For such then was Evangeline Musset created, a Dame

of lofty Lineage, who, in the early eighties, had discarded her family Tandem, in which her Mother and Father found Pleasure enough, for the distorted Amusement of riding all smack-of-astride, like any Yeoman going to gather in his Crops ; and with much jolting and galloping, was made, hour by hour, less womanly, " Though never", said she, " has that Greek Mystery occurred to me, which is known as the Dashing out of the Testicles, and all that goes with it !" Which is said to have happened to a Byzantine Baggage of the Trojan Period, more to her Surprise than her Pleasure. Yet it is an agreeable Circumstance that the Ages thought fit to hand down this Miracle, for Hope springs eternal in the human Breast.

It has been noted by some and several, that Women have in them the Pip of Romanticism so well grown and fat of Sensibility, that they, upon reaching an uncertain Age, discard Duster, Offspring and Spouse, and a little after are seen leaning, all of a limp, on a Pillar of Bathos.

Evangeline Musset was not one of these, for she had been developed in the Womb of her most gentle Mother to be a Boy, when therefore, she came forth an Inch or so less than this, she paid no Heed to the Error, but donning a Vest of a superb Blister and Tooling, a Belcher for tippet and a pair of hip-boots with a scarlet channel (for it was a most wet wading) she took her Whip in hand, calling her Pups about her, and so set out upon the Road of Destiny, until such time as they should grow to be Hounds of a Blood, and Pointers with a certainty in the

Butt of their Tails ; waiting patiently beneath Cypresses for this Purpose, and under the Boughs of the aloe tree, composing, as she did so, Madrigals to all sweet and ramping things.

Her Father, be it known, spent many a windy Eve pacing his Library in the most normal of Night-Shirts, trying to think of ways to bring his erring Child back into that Religion and Activity which has ever been thought sufficient for a Woman ; for already, when Evangeline appeared at Tea to the Duchess Clitoressa of Nates-court, women in the way (the Bourgeoise be it noted, on an errand to some nice Church of the Catholic Order, with their Babes at Breast, and Husbands at Arm) would snatch their Skirts from Contamination, putting such wincing Terror into their Dears with their quick and trembling Plucking, that it had been observed, in due time, by all Society, and Evangeline was in order of becoming one of those who is spoken to out of Generosity, which her Father could see, would by no Road, lead her to the Altar.

He had Words with her enough, saying : " Daughter, daughter, I perceive in you most fatherly Sentiments. What am I to do ?"   And she answered him High enough, "Thou, good Governor, wast expecting a Son when you lay atop of your Choosing, why then be so mortal wounded when you perceive that you have your Wish ?   Am I not doing after your very Desire, and is it not the more commendable, seeing that I do it without the Tools for the Trade, and yet nothing complain ?"

In the days of which I write she had come to be a witty and learned Fifty, and though most short of Stature and nothing handsome, was so much in Demand, and so wide famed for her Genius at bringing up by Hand, and so noted and esteemed for her Slips of the Tongue that it finally brought her into the Hall of Fame, where she stood by a Statue of Venus as calm as you please, or leaned upon a lacrymal Urn with a small Sponge for such as Wept in her own Time and stood in Need of it.

Thus begins this Almanack, which all Ladies should carry about with them, as the Priest his Breviary, as the Cook his Recipes, as the Doctor his Physic, as the Bride her Fears, and as the Lion his Roar !

# JANUARY *hath 31 days*

---

THIS be the first Month of our Christian calendar, when the Earth is bound and the Seas in the grip of Terror. When the Birds give no Evidence of themselves, and are in the Memory alone recorded, when the Sap lies sleeping and the Tree knows nothing of it, when the bright Herbage and flourishing green things are only hope, when the Plough is put away with the Harrow, and the Fields give their Surface to a Harvest of Snow, which no Sickle garners, and for which no Grange languishes, and which never weighs the home-going Cart of the Farmer, but sows itself alone and reaps itself unrecorded.

Now in this Month, as it is with Mother Earth, so it will appear it is with all things of Nature, and most especially Woman.

For in this Month she is a little pitiful for what she has made of man, and what she has throughout the Ages, led him to expect, cultivating him indeed to such a Pitch that she is somewhat responsible.

Patience Scalpel was of this Month, and belongs to this Almanack for one Reason only, that from Beginning to End, Top to Bottom, inside and out, she could not understand Women and their Ways as they were about her, above her and before her.

She saw them gamboling on the Greensward, she heard them pinch and moan within the Gloom of many a stately Mansion ; she beheld them floating across the Ceilings, (for such was Art in the old Days), diapered in *Toile de Jouy*, and welded without Flame, in one incalculable Embrace. "And what", she said, "the silly Creatures may mean by it is more than I can diagnose ! I am of my Time my Time's best argument, and who am I that I must die in my Time, and never know what it is in the Whorls and Crevices of my Sisters so prolongs them to the bitter End ? Do they not have Organs as exactly alike as two Peas, or twin Griefs ; and are they not eclipsed ever so often with the galling Check-rein of feminine Tides ? So what to better Purpose than to sit the Dears on a Stack of Blotters, and let it go at that, giving them in their meantime a Bible and a Bobbin, and say with all Pessimism—they have come to a blind Alley ; there will be no Children born for a Season, and what matter it ?"

Thus her Voice was heard throughout the Year, as cutting in its Derision as a surgical Instrument, nor did she use it to come to other than a Day and yet another Day in which she said, " I have tried all means, Mathematical, Poetical, Statistical and Reasonable, to come to the Core of this Distemper, known as Girls ! Girls ! And can nowhere find where a Woman got the Account that makes her such a deft Worker at the Single Beatitude. Who gave her the Directions for it, the necessary Computation and Turpitude ? Where, and in what dark Chamber was the Tree so cut of Life, that the Branch turned to the Branch, and made of the Cuttings a Garden of Ecstasy ?"

Merry Laughter rose about her, as Doll Furious was seen in ample dimity, sprigged with Apple Blossom, footing it fleetly after the proportionless Persuasions of Señorita Fly-About, one of Buzzing Much to Rome !

" In my time", said Patience Scalpel, "Women came to enough trouble by lying abed with the Father of their Children. What then in this good Year of our Lord has paired them like to like, with never a Beard between them, layer for layer, were one to unpack them to the very Ticking ? Methinks", she mused, her

Starry Eyes aloft, where a Peewit was yet content to mate it hot among the Branches, making for himself a Covey in the olden Formula, "they love the striking Hour, nor would breed the Moments that go to it. Sluts !" she said pleasantly after a little thought, "Are good Mothers to supply them with Luxuries in the next Generation ; for they them- selves will have no Shes, unless some Her puts them forth ! Well I'm not the Woman for it ! They well have to pluck where they may. My Daughters shall go amarry- ing !"

# FEBRUARY *hath 29 days*

---

**T**HIS be a Love Letter for a Present, and when she is Catched, what shall I do with her ? God knows ! For 'tis safe to say I do not, and what we know

## SAINTS DAYS

**T**HESE are the Days on which Dame Musset was sainted, and for these things.

*January*

When new whelped, she

not, is our only proof of Him !

My Love she is an Old Girl, out of Fashion, Bugles at the Bosom, and theredown a much Thumbed Mystery and a Maze. She doth jangle with last Year's attentions, she is melted with Death's Fire ! Then what shall I for her that hath never been accomplished ? It is a very Parcel of Perplexities ! Shall one stumble on a Nuance that twenty Centuries have not pounced upon, yea worried and made a Kill of ? Hath not her Hair of old been braided with the Stars ? Her shin half-circled by the Moon. Hath she not been turned all ways that the Sands of her Desire know all Runnings ? Who can make a New Path where there be no Wilderness ? In the Salt Earth lie Parcels of lost Perfection—surely I shall not loosen her Straps a New Way, Love hath been too long a Time ! Will she unpack her Panels for such a Stale Receipt, pour out her Treasures for a

was found to have missed by an Inch.

*February*

When but five, she lamented Mid-prayers, that the girls in the Bible were both Earth-hushed and Jew-touched forever and ever.

*March*

When nine she learned how the Knee termed Housemaid's is come by, when the Slavy was bedridden at the turn of the scullery and needed a kneeling-to.

*April*

When fast on fifteen she hushed a Near-Bride with the left Flounce of her Ruffle that her Father in sleeping might not know of the oh !

*May*

When sweet twenty-one prayed upon her past Bearing she went to the Cockpit and crowed with the best. And at the Full of the Moon in Gaiters and Gloves mooed with the Herd, her Heels with their Hoofs, and in the wet Dingle hooted for hoot with the Quail on the Spinney, calling for Brides Wing and a Feather to flock with.

*June*

When well thirty, she, like

coin worn thin ? Yet to renounce her were a thing as old ; and saying "Go !" but shuts the Door that hath banged a million Years !

Oh Zeus ! Oh Diane ! Oh Hellebore ! Oh Absalom ! Oh Piscary Right ! What shall I do with it ! *To have been the First*, that alone would have gifted me ! As it is, shall I not pour ashes upon my Head, gird me in Sackcloth, covering my Nothing and Despair under a Mountain of Cinders, and thus become a Monument to No-Ability for her sake ?

Verily, I shall place me before her Door, and when she cometh forth I shall think she has left her Feet inward upon the Sill and when she enters in, I shall dream her Hands be yet outward upon the Door—for therein is no way for me, and Fancy is my only Craft.

★

all Men before her, made a Harlot a good Woman by making her Mistress.

*July*

When forty she bayed up a Tree whose Leaves had no Turning and whose Name was Florella.

*August*

When fifty odd and a day she came upon that Wind that is labelled the second.

*Septembre*

When sixty some, she came to no Good as well as another.

*October*

When Sixty was no longer a Lodger of hers, she bought a Pair of extra faroff, and ultra near-to Opera Glasses, and carried them always in a Sac by her Side.

*November*

When eighty-eight she said, "It's a Hook Girl, not a Button, you should know your Dress better."

*December*

When just before her last Breath she ordered a Pasty and let a Friend eat it, renouncing the World and its Pitfalls like all Saints before her, when she had no longer Room for them.

Prosit !

# MARCH *hath 31 days*

A MONG such Dames of which we write, were two British Women. One was called Lady Buck-and-Balk, and the other plain Tilly-Tweed-In-Blood. Lady Buck-and-Balk sported a Monocle and believed in Spirits. Tilly-Tweed-In-Blood sported a Stetson, and believed in Marriage. They came to the Temple of the Good Dame Musset, and they sat to Tea, and this is what they said :

"Just because woman falls, in this Age, to Woman, does that mean that we are not to recognize Morals ? What has England done to legalize these Passions ? Nothing ! Should she not be brought to Task, that never once through her gloomy Weather have two dear Doves been seen approaching in their bridal Laces, to pace, in stately Splendor up the Altar Aisle, there to be United in Similarity, under mutual Vows of Loving, Honouring, and Obeying, while the One and the Other fumble in that nice Temerity, for the equal gold Bands that shall make of one a Wife, and the other a Bride ?

"Most wretchedly never that I have heard of, nor one such Pair seen later in a Bed of Matrimony, tied up in their best Ribands, all under a Canopy of Cambric, Bosom to Bosom, Braid to Braid, Womb to Womb ! But have, ever since the instigation of that Alliance, lain abed out of Wedlock, sinning in a double and similar Sin ; rising unprovided for by Church or Certificate ; Fornicating in an Evil so exactly of a piece, that the Judgement Call must be answered in a Trembling Tandem !"

"Therefore we think to bring the Point to the Notice of our Judges, and have it set before the House of Lords. For when a Girl falls in Love, with no matter what, should she not be protected in some way, from Hazard, ever attending that which is illegal ? And should One or the Other stray, ought there not to be a Law as binding upon her as upon another, that Alimony might be

Collected ; and that Straying be nipped in the Bud ?"

"Tis a thought" said the Good Musset. "But then there are Duels to take the place of the Law, and there's always a Way out, should one or both be found wanting. A strong Gauntlet struck lightly athwart the Buttock would bring her to the common Green, where with Rapier, or Fowling-Piece, she might demand and take her Satisfaction, thus ending it for both, in one way or another."

"It is not enough," said Lady Buck-and-Balk. "Think how tender are the Hearts of Women, at their toughest ! One small Trickle of Blood on that dear Torso (and here she starved toward her choice) and I should be less than any Man ! And I dare say Tilly would be as distracted were she to perceive in me one Rib gone astray, or one Wrist most horribly bleeding ! Nay, we could never come to a Killing, for women have not, like brutal Man," she concluded, "and Death between them, but Pity only, and a resuscitating Need ! Like may not spit Like, nor Similarity sit in Inquest upon Similarity !"

"I could do it with most disconcerting Ease," said Dame Musset, "but then there is in me no Wren's Blood or Trepidation. Why should a Woman be un-spit ? Love of Woman for Woman should increase Terror. I see that so far it does not. All is not as it should be !"

"Ah never, never, never," sighed a soft Voice, and the trio thus became aware of that touch of Sentiment known as Masie Tuck-and-Frill, erstwhile *Sage-femme* but now, because of the Trend of the Times, lamentably out of a Job, though it was said, nothing could cure her

of her Longing, for though she was called to no Beds, but
those of Sisters mingled in the Bond of no Relativity,
nevertheless looked with a hoping Eye between the Sheets,
and put a loving Hand at the Crook of every Arm, and
between the Knees, though she found nothing ever requir-
ing Attention, nor any small Voice saying "Where am I ?"
she still cherished a fond Delusion that in one Way or
another, the Pretties would yet whelp a little Sweet, by
fair Means or foul, and was heard in many a dim Corridor
admonishing a Love of nine Months not to overtake
her strength, and to be particularly careful not to slip in
going down Stairs.   "For", as she said, "Creation has ever
been too Marvellous for us to doubt of it now, and though
the Medieval way is still thought good enough, what is to
prevent some modern Girl from rising from the Couch of
a Girl as modern, with something new in her Mind ?   To
stick to the old Tradition is Credulity, and Credulity has
been worn to a Thread.  A Feather", she said, "might
accomplish it, or a Song rightly sung, or an Exclamation
said in the right Place, or a Trifle done in the right Spirit,
and then you would have need of me indeed!" and here she
began to sing the first Lullaby ever cast for a Girl's Girl
should she one day become a Mother.  And with this
as a Preface, every Woman of every sort, found her Eve-
rywhere.  So it was that the Three saw her sitting among
the Cushions sewing a fine Seam, and saying in the Wist-
ful, lost Voice of those with a Trade too tender for Oblivion, "Women are a little this side of Contemplation,
their Love has the Poignancy of all lost Tension.  Men

are too early, Women too tardy, and Religion too late for Religion.

"Love in Man is Fear of Fear. Love in Woman is Hope without Hope. Man fears all that can be taken from him, a Woman's Love includes that, and then Lies down beside it. A Man's love is built to fit Nature. Woman's is a Kiss in the Mirror. It is a Farewell to the Creator, without disturbing him, the supreme Tenderness toward Oblivion, Battle after Retreat, Challenge when the Sword is broken. Yea, it strikes loudly on the Heart, for thus she gives her Body to all unrecorded Music, which is the Psalm."

"You speak," said Dame Musset, turning a charmed Eye upon her, "in the Voice of one who should be One of Us !"

"I speak", said Masie Tuck-and-Frill, "in that Voice which has been accorded ever to those who go neither Hither nor Thither ; the Voice of the Prophet. Those alone who sit in one Condition, their Life through, know what the plans were, and what the Hopes are, and where the Spot the two lie, in that Rot you call your Lives. Time goes with the Beast also, the Centuries fold him down, the Cry of his Young comes upward about him, the sigh of his Elders is as high as his Horns, yet above his Horns is also a Voice crying "Too hoo ! I would," she added, "that the Mind's Eye had not been so bent upon the Heart."

"It's a good Place," said Dame Musset in a Tone advertising her a Person well pleased a long time.

"A good place indeed," returned Masie Tuck-and-Frill, "but a better when seen Indirectly."

"I", said Lady Buck-and-Balk—for Spirits had made her a little Callous to Nuance, "would that we could do away with Man altogether !"

"It cannot be," sighed Tilly Tweed-in-Blood, "we need them for carrying of Coals, lifting of Beams, and things of one kind or another."

"Ah the dears !" said Patience Scalpel, that moment bounding in upon them, divesting herself of her furs, "and is there one hereabouts ?"

"Most certainly not !" cried Lady Buck-and-Balk in one Breath with Tilly Tweed-in-Blood, as if a large Mouse had run over their Shins, "What a thing to say !"

"Oh Fie, and why not !" said Patience sipping a cognac. "Were it not for them, you would not be half so pleased with things as they are. Delight is always a little running of the Blood in Channels astray !"

"When I wish to contemplate the highest Pitch to which Irony has climbed, and when I really desire to *wallow* in impersonal Tragedy", said Dame Musset, "I think of that day, forty years ago, when I, a Child of ten, was deflowered by the Hand of a Surgeon ! I, even I, came to it as other Women, and I never a Woman before nor since !"

"Oh my Darling !" wailed Tilly, in an Anguish on the sec-

## ZODIAC

THIS is the part about Heaven that has never been told. After the Fall of Satan (and as he fell, Lucifer uttered a loud

ond. My poor, dear betrayed mishandled Soul ! To think of it ! Why I don't know whom to strike first ! But someone shall suffer for it I tell you. These Eyes shall know no Sleep until you are revenged !"

"Peace !" said Dame Musset, putting a Hand upon her Wrist, "I am my Revenge !"

"I had not thought of that," said Tilly happily, "You have, verily, hanged, cut down, and re-hung Judas a thousand times !"

"And shall again, please God !" said Dame Musset.

"That Man's Hand," said Patience Scalpel, "must drip more Agony and Regret than the Hand of Lady Macbeth, and must burn hotter than a Serpent's Tongue !"

"He mutters in his Sleep," said Tuck-and-Frill," and turns from Side to Side, and finds no Comfort !"

"He be one Man," said Dame Musset peacefully, "who does not brag."

Cry, heard from one End of Forever-and-no-end to the other), all the Angels, Aries, Taurus, Gemini, Cancer, Leo, Virgo, Libra, Scorpio, Sagittarius, Capricornus, Aquarius, Pisces, all, all gathered together, so close that they were not recognizable, one from the other. And not nine Months later, there was heard under the Dome of Heaven a great Crowing, and from the Midst, an Egg, as incredible as a thing forgotten, fell to Earth, and striking, split and hatched, and from out of it stepped one saying "Pardon me, I must be going !" And this was the first Woman born with a Difference.

After this the Angels parted, and on the Face of each was the Mother look.

Why was that ?

★

# APRIL *hath 30 days*

---

## THEIR SIGNS :

**A**CUTE Melancholy is noticeable in those who have gone a long Way into this Matter, whereas a light giggling, dancing Fancy seems to support those in the very first Stages ; brief of Thought ; cut of Concentra-

tion; a Tendency to hop, skip and jump, and to misplace
the Eye at every single or several Manifestation of Girl
in like Distemper.

Chill succeeds, and Restlesness at Night, or unaccount-
able Tabulation of unimportant Objects, such as Flag-
Stones (Busbys an she be in London !) Steeples, Mulber-
ries in Baskets, Tabs to Dresses, Hooves to Horses, and
Stars in the Sky.

This gives place, in from six to eight Weeks, to a So-
briety that includes thoughts of Transmigration, Levita-
tion, Myopia and Blight. The Eye trickles, the Breath
is short, the Spleen is distended, and the Epiglottis rises
and falls like the continual swallowing of the Heart.
Whereupon the Veins are seen to lift themselves, the Nerves
twitch, the Palms become moist, the Feet lose their
activity, the Bowels contract, and, as in the old Days when
a Person in the last stages of Hydrophobia sometimes found
small Whelps in the Urine, in the Waters of such is seen
the fully Robed on-marching Figure of Venus no larger
than a Caraway Seed, a Trident in one Hand and a
Gos-Wasp on the left Fist.

One such, in the Death Agony, is said to have passed
a whole School of Trulls, couched on a Conch Shell, which
such, emitting Fire, raged until they had brought the
Body of the Fluid to such Flame in its Night Vase, that it
resembled a burning Brandy, and so ran upon the Suffer-
er that she was seen to be re-entered in a burst of Smoke,
and was thus, in less than a Second, a charred and glowing
Ember. Be this as it may, there have been some and sev-

eral who hold the Sickness and the Signs of such are diverse to the Point where Classification becomes almost impossible ; an whole Anatomy would needs be penned to get at so much as the smallest Tendril of the Malady, Grief and Agony.

Others be of a Temper that nothing will discountenance them save Vanity. These are seen twining Ivy in their Hair, or dashing a Sprig of Bay athwart the Temples, while intoning, " I am I !" nor deigning to have Trouble whatsoever, unless someone demand " What of it ?" which does send them into such a Fury that the very Raiment of their Company is in Danger, and so distorted are their Faces by bootless Pride, that they resemble, in no small degree, the Wolf despoiled of her Litter.

Still others are of a different Dye, and are sweet and tender always, and find much Pleasure in making Sacrifices and Gifts, and in strewing Roses before the oncoming of their Adored. In such one sees the limpid Eye, the up-curved Mouth, the silken Child's Hair, the *bonne mine*, the regnant Temper, the strong Heart and the Courage that goes for Folly. Such can be counted on at all hours, and are buried when dead, with the look of the good Clock which has been never slow or fast, but has tolled the exact hour for the duration of Mortality, and is silenced only and unrecording, for that the Lord put forth his Shears and cut down the Weights.

# MAY *hath 31 days*

SWEET May stood putting on her last venereal Touches while Patience Scalpel held forth in that divine and ethereal Voice for which she was noted, the Voice of one whose Ankles are nibbled by the Cherubs, while amid the Rugs Dame Musset brought Doll Furious to a certainty.

"What", said Patience Scalpal, "can you women see in each other ?   Where is the Parting of the Ways and the Horseman that hunts ?   Where", she reflected, "there is Prostitution and Drunkeness, there is bound to be Immorality, or I do not count the Times, but what is this ?"

"And", said Dame Musset, rising in Bed, "that's all there is, and there is no more !"

"But oh !" cried Doll.

"Down Woman", said Dame Musset in her friendliest, "there may be a mustard seed !"

Now the sisters Nip and Tuck, two hearty Lasses who claimed all of Spain as their Torment, knocking on the Shutters, were let in. "We come", said they "to let you know there is a Flail loose in the Town who is crying from Corner to Niche, in that lamenting Herculean Voice that sounds to us like a Sister lost, for certainly it is not the Whine of Motherhood, but a more mystic, sodden Sighing. So it seems to us, as Members of the Sect, we should deliver to you this piece of Information, that you may repair what has never been damaged."

"It shall be done, and done most wily well", said the Dame, buckling on her Four-in-hand, and clapping her Busby athwart her roguish Knee, "Where was she last seen, and which way going ?"

"She was ramping in the Bois", said Nip, "and tearing through the Champs Elysées," said Tuck, "and was last seen in a Cloud of Dust, hot foot after an historic Fact."

"A grain, a grain !" lamented Doll.

"She shall be thrown", said Dame Musset, regarding

not, "and well branded, i' the Bottom, Flank, or Buttocks-boss.   To scent, we will chase her into a very Tan-
gle of Temptation !"

Now who was it these good Women hunted but Bounding Bess, noted for her Enthusiasm in things forgotten, and
having paced it ably up the dusty Lengths of the Elysées, they suddenly came upon her, compounding Maxims
by the Wayside.   She was grand at History, and nothing
short of magnificent at Concentration, so it was that the
Sisters Nip and Tuck and the good Saint Musset came to a
Pause, and she nowise aware of them, saying to herself
(for who ever held that Soliloquy was for Hamlet alone ?)
"There have been great Women in History and though
now they face upward, they have me to repine.   Not the
least of these was somewhat turned to Love.   The good
Catherine of Russia thought nothing of twittering over a
Man at ten, and at twelve thundering down Diderot, or
some as fine, and in like manner was not Sappho herself,
though given to singing over the limp Bodies of Girls like
any noisy Nightingale, nevertheless held in great Respect by
the philosophers of her time ?   Therefore if I sense in
myself a tendency to that Trifle of Craft known hereabouts as Miss Spiritus, who sings Psalms for the Rosi-
crucians, or whatever that new Cult may be, why should I,
in yielding to that Impulse, necessarily come a Cropper,
and be found witless and wanting, though laid all of a
Stretch on some enchanting Green ? One can but try !
Nay, but I think it a Chance in a million to prove, no mat-

ter what the Mount, that one may come down well enough in one's Wits, to yet be taken seriously when discussing the Destiny of Nations."

"That woman's Feet", said Dame Musset, in that hard, practical and clear Voice, which has been heard coming from all Lungs the World over, an they blow in a Spartan Chest, "are all Heels, and what do they ever portend but a pedant. They are always gaited thus, and know not whether they are walking into or out of Truth. She is not for us !" and so saying, she cracked her Whip against her Boot, turning toward a Pasty Shop hard by, Nip at her Heels, but sensing a short Sound in the Herd, the Dame turned back, there to behold (as was her Custom) Miss Tuck seated a little too close to History, or whatever it was that Bounding Bess radiated, and toying, in that brief Second, with minor Details that went as far back as the Fall of Rome.

"She is, has been, and ever will be," said Miss Nip, "a darling Detriment to Sleep and Sequence, and will, no doubt, come home as riddled as a Medlar, resembling, in no small degree, the first Round of a Butcher's Picnic, or the premier Half of a Trunk Murder, for that Girl," she said pleasantly, "has in her a trifle of Terrier Blood, and must be forever worrying at every Petticoat as ever dangled over a Hip in this our time !"

"Tis a blessing," commented Dame Musset, selecting two of the happiest combinations in Cake, "that some of us are mortal and must suffer Death. The Future needs it, as we need Sleep. I live," she added, "for two remaining Ferocities, Food and Understanding !"

"Tell me about it !" said Nip, for she was at best
a little curious, being hard pressed by Journalism, and
could not let a Morsel go, though she knew well that
it could be printed nowhere and in no Country, for Life
is represented in no City by a Journal dedicated to the
Undercurrents, or for that matter to any real Fact
whatsoever.

" In my day," said Dame Musset, and at once the look
of the Pope, which she carried about with her as a Habit,
waned a little, and there was seen to shine forth the Cunning of a Monk in Holy Orders, in some Counry too old for
Tradition," in my day I was a Pioneer and a Menace, it was
not then as it is now, *chic* and pointless to a degree, but
as daring as a Crusade, for where now it leaves a woman
talkative, so that we have not a Secret among us, then
it left her in Tears and Trepidation.  Then one had to
lure them to the Breast, and now," she said, " You have to
smack them, back and front to ween them at all ! What joy
has the missionary," she added, her Eyes narrowing and
her long Ears moving with Disappointment, " when all the
Heathen greet her with Glory Halleluja ! before she opens
her Mouth, and with an Amen ! before she shuts it !  I
would," she said, " that there were one Woman somewhere
that one could take to task for Lethargy. Ah !" she
sighed, " there were many such when I was a Girl, and in
particular I recall one dear old Countess who was not to
be convinced until I, fervid with Truth, had finally so floor-
ed her in every capacious Room of that dear ancestral

Home, that I knew to a Button, how every Ticking was made ! And what a lack of Art there is in the Upholstery Trade, for that they do not finish off the under Parts of Sofas and Chairs with anything like the Elegance showered upon that Portion which comes to the Eye ! There should," she added, with a touch of that committee strain which flowed in a deep wide Stream in her Sister, "be Trade for Contacts, guarding that on which the Lesbian Eye must, in its March through Life, rest itself. I would not, however." she said, "have it understood that I yearn with any very great Vastness for the early eighties ; then Girls were as mute as a Sampler, and as importunate as a War, and would have me lay on, charge and retreat the night through, as if," she finished, "a Woman, be she ever so good of Intention and a Martyr, could wind herself upon one Convert, and still find Strength in the Nape of her Neck for the next. Still," she remarked, sipping a little hot tea, "they were dear Creatures, and they have paced me to a contented and knowing fifty. I am well pleased. Upon my Sword there is no Rust, and upon my Escutcheon so many Stains that I have, in this manner, created my own Banner and my own Badge. I have learned on the Bodies of all Women, all Customs, and from their Minds have all Nations given up their Secrets. I know that the Orientals are cold to the Waist, and from there flame with a mighty and quick crackling Fire. I have learned that Anglo Saxons thaw slowly but that they thaw from Head to Heel, and so it is with their Minds. The Asiatic is warm and willing, and goes out like a Fire-

cracker ; the Northerner is cool and cautious, but
burns and burns, until," she said reminiscently, "you see
that Candle lit by you in youth, burning about your Bier
in Death. It is time now that I find me a Night-
light, and just what Fusion of Bloods it be, I have not as
yet determined, but—I think I have found it."

"Where !" exclaimed Nip, looking about her with a
touch of kindly Apprehension.

"The Night-Light of Love," said Saint Musset,
"burns I think me in the slightly muted Crevices of all
Women who have been a little sprung with continual
playing of the Spring Song, though I may be mistaken,
for be it known, I have not yet made certain on this Point.
There is one such in our midst on whom I have had
a Weather Eye these many Years.  She is a little concocted of one bad night in Venice and one sly Woman going
to morning Mass, her Name is writ from here to Sicily,
as Cynic Sal.  She dressed like a Coachman of the period of Pecksniff, but she drives an empty Hack.  And that
is one Woman," she said, "who shall yet find me as Fare,
and if at the Journey's end, she still cracks as sharp a
Whip, and has never once descended the Drivers's Seat
to put her Head within to see what rumpled meaning
there sits, why she may sing for her Pains, I shall get off
at London and find me another who has somewhat of a
budding Care for a Passenger."

"Be she not the Woman," said Nip flightily, "who
is of so vain and jealous a Nature that do what you will
you cannot please her, and mention this or that, she is not

contented ? For if it be the one, she has passed through my ken as Timid Tom, or Most-Infirm-of-Purpose."

"It may be," said Dame Musset, "and it may not."

"How true that is when 'tis said of a Woman," acknowledged Nip ; "no Man could be both one and neither like to us, and now," she said "I see Miss Tuck this way wending, hot and hunting, and I think me she stands in Need of a fal-lal or two in the shape of a Sandwich, and a dish of Tea, for she has the look to me of one who has laid Waste a barren Land. That pathetic Expression one occasionally observes on the Faces of our younger, less acute Generation ; her under Lip doth hang with a Dexterity that has found no Thanks."

"Ah Woe is me !" sighed Miss Tuck, seating herself at the Table, and leaning upon a tiny pocket Handkerchief, "you, my dear Musset were, as always, quite right. She thaws nothing but Facts, do what I would, nor one unfathomed Mystery in the Lot ! Nor alas, one gentle Fancy · such as sends the Pigeon up among his Feathers, nay, nor one Crumb untabulated, be it ever so infinitesimal. For no matter what I came upon but that Wench had some Word for it ! Now it was Horace, now it was Spinoza, and yet again it was the Descent of Man," she shuddered, "and that Descent," said she in a dreadful Whisper, "I will have nothing to do with, here or then ! When a Woman is as well seasoned in her every Joint as she, with exact and enduring Knowledge, there is nothing for it but to let her add herself up to an impossible Zero, and so come to her Death of that premeditated Accuracy, but then," she said, putting a soft little Hand into that of Miss Nip, "you know how fast I recover, and how many Hours there are in a Day."

"Some women", said Dame Musset, "are Sea-Cattle, and some are Land-Hogs, and yet others are Worms crawling about our Almanacks, but some," she said, "are Sisters of Heaven, and these we must follow and not be side-tracked."

"How am I to help it if I go astray," cried Miss Tuck, "when every Law of Love and Desire was long ago as mixed as a Contortion of Traffic ? I do not know a blind Alley from a Boulevard, nor a Cross-Road to what it may be running to, and Sign-Posts never serve for anything but unsettling my Mind !"

"You," cut in Miss Nip, "would follow, all panting and blind with good Intentions, the Trail of a Field Mouse! There is no Land so uncharterd of Trails but you would find a Ribbon of Comfort even in the Desert, and lead yourself, by your very Fury of Willingness, into a Wallow of Trouble before Sundown !"  "Oh God, don't I know it !" sobbed Tuck.

✶

# JUNE *hath 30 days*

## PORTENTS, SIGNS AND OMENS

WHEN Infant Grundy rises like the Sickle
The dying Grundy will her nothing stickle,
But wane upon this World of Odds and Omen,
The newer Prudy waxing for the Women,

For to a Woman shall a Woman stoop
When she had birched them well about the Coop,
And nowhere else, as they have done ere this ;
No Man shall nip them, and no Boy shall kiss,
No Lad shall hoist them gaily Heels o'er Head
Nor lay them 'twixt his Breast-bone and his Bed.
Nor flay them with sweet Portent and with Sign.
Nor reap their Image tiny in this Eyen.
Nay, this shall never be their earthly Cost
But, all unlike the Bird of Memory lost,
Late roosting on the Hollow tree of Time,
Which only backward can the Scaler climb,
They by themselves mislaid shall be, God wot,
Binding this Nonsense to a finer Knot,
Casting to the Winds all common Care
Like a Bell that throws its Nature to the Air.
Of such is then the high and gaming Pride
Of Woman by a Woman's girlish Side !

★

# THE FOURTH GREAT MOMENT OF HISTORY

IN the time of Heat, when the Flowers bloom and the Birds sing and the Squirrels burn, and Man turns inside out for Love, Dame Musset, like many a Dandy with his Candytufts of Hope and his Gallipots of Love, or like a Grig of a Rip with his Foxglove and Fustian, had also an Eye when she went out for a Walk.

The Luxembourg boasted no Hedge or Statue that had proportions or density sufficient to make Hide of a Petticoat, for Musset knew them to a Turn and a Twig. Therefore she was no little surprised when one mellow Sunday, she in walking out with Doll on her Arm (Musset deeming indeed that she had managed most neatly this matter of Bushes and Nooks), heard Doll going about it thus : "My most Darling, but now has come the Time when you must listen to the fourth great Moment of History (having undoubtedly heard the other three), which is of Sheba and Jezebel.  So though I be neither Sheba nor you good Jezebel, we are exactly lesser, so but give Ear.

" Jezebel, that flighty forthright, used to spend much of her Time in angling from her Window and crying 'Uoo Hoo ! ' to the Kings that way wending to War and to Death.  And some turned in at her Door, and others went on, though not a many ' tis true.  Thus was Jezebel employed, when the Queen of Sheba passed beneath her Window, and Jezebel leaning outward called 'Uoo Hooo !'

"*And that was Jezebel's last 'Uoo Hoo !'*"
Musset's Eyes fell.

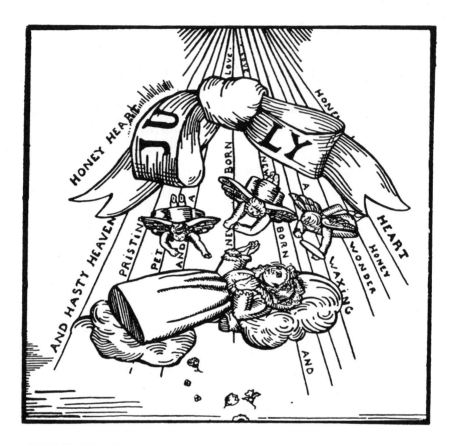

# JULY *hath 31 days*

THE Time has come, when, with unwilling Hand,
I must set down what a woman says to a Woman
and she be up to her Ears in Love's Acre.   Should
we not like to think it, at least if not of poetic Value,
then strophed to a Romanesque Fortitude, as clipped of
Foliage as a British Hedge, or at least as fitting to the thing

it covers as an Infant's Cap, which even when frilled to the very frontal Bone, and taking into account the most pulsing Suture, is somewhat of a Head's proportion, nor flows and drips away and adown, as if it were no Covering for probability ?

Nay, nowhere, in all the fulsome data of most uncovered and naked backrunning of Nature, nor in the Columns of our most jaundiced Journals, can be gathered the vaguest Idea of the Means by which she puts her Heart from her Mouth to her Sleeve, and from her Sleeve into Rhetorick, and from that into the Ear of her beloved. To the Ancients, Love Letters and Love Hearsay (though how much Luck and how much Cunning this was on the part of the Outrunners in the Thickets of prehistoric proability, none can say, for doubt me not but from Fish to Man there has been much Back-mating and Front to Front, though only a Twitter of it comes out of the Past) were from like to unlike. Our own Journals teem with Maids and their Beards, whose very highest encomiums reach no more glorious Foothold than "Honey Lou", or "Snooky dear", or "my great big beautiful bedridden Doll," whose Turnabout it would seem, is only one side proper to the Lord. But hear how a Maid goes at a Maid : "And are you well my own ? But tell me hastily, are you well ? for I am well, oh most newly well, and well again. And if all's well, then ends we all ends up ! But if you be about to be nowise probable but tell me, and I will burst my Gussets with hereditary Weeping, that we be not dated to a Moon and are apart

by dint of diddling Nature, and parting is such sweet
Sorrow ! How all too oft are we but one in our Team !
So tell me if you but be well for well I be !"

Or such Words as this : " I may have trifled in my
Day, or in Days to come, or today itself ; or even now be
rifling Hours for the penning of this to you, but though
I gather dear Daffodils abroad, plunge Head first into
many a Parsley Field, tamper with high strung and low
lying ; though I press to my Bosom the very Flower
of Women, or tire myself to a prostrate Portion, without
a Breath between me and her ; toss her over the off-leg
to bring her to rights, say never that I do not adore you
as my only and my best. To her I give but a Phoenix
Hour, she is but the hone to my blunt, which shall Toledo
to you. To you I give my Bays, my Laurels, my Ever-
lastings, my Peonies, my hardy Perennials and my early
percipient Posies, that bloom for such effulgence as shines
alone from your Countenance ! (Viz., to wit : were she
haggard, gray, toothless, torn, deformed, damned, evil,
putrid and no one's Pleasure ; or if on the other Hand she
were lovely, straight, marble browed, red in her bloom,
bright in the Eye, headed with Hair, and Venused to
boot —'tis all one to a Girl in Love !) For you alone I re-
serve that Gasp under Gasp, that Sigh behind Sigh, that
Attention back of feigned ; that Cloud's Silver is yours —
take it ! What care I on whom it rains ! The real me is
your real yours, I can spend myself in Hedgerow and Coun-
ter-patch, 'tis only the Dust of my reality, the Smoke that
tells of the Fire, which my own Darling Lamb, my most

perfect and tirelessly different, is yours, I am thine !
You compel me. !"

Compels her ! Yea, though the Recipient be as torpid
as a Mohammedan after his hundredth Ramadan, as tempe-
rate as a Frost in Timgad, as stealthy as a Bishop without
a Post, still and yet, and how again it will command her ;
so encore. Were it of as good a quality and as sharp as
Madagascar Pepper, Still it commands her, it can command
her up-stairs and down, right side and wrong, peek-a-boo,
or all fronts-face, in Mid-moon and Mad-night, in Dawn,
in Day, yea, still it will command her, so pricked is she with
longing, and so primed to a Breath, that should her
Honey-heart hang mincemeat Tartlets about her Waist for
a Girdle, would she preen to the Pie, and clap with Delight ; or should she be ordered to wear a Wig backward,
with its curl well over her Nose, still she would do it, a
Lamb both fore and aft and all at the one look, saying :
"You know my quick Step, my real Run, my true Bite.
My intake and withdraw are at your behest, I am but a
Shade of myself an I am not by your Side, and what I
am is because you are, and should you turn and not
find me, it is because I have taken that not worthy of
you to another, who may blow me bright again to shine
toward your Lightning, a Sun to my Beam !"

Nay— —I cannot write it ! It is worse than this !
More dripping, more lush, more lavender, more mid-
mauve, more honeyed, more Flower-casting, more Cher-
ub-bound, more downpouring, more saccharine, more
lamentable, more gruesomely unmindful of Reason or

Sense, to say nothing of Humor.  Nowhere, and in no Pocket, do such keep a Seed of the fit on which to sneeze themselves into the fitting, they be not happy unless writhing in Treacle, and like a trapped Fly, crawl through cardinal Morasses, all Legs tethered and dragging in the Gum of Love !

And just as some others are foul of Tongue, these are sweet to sickness.  One sickens the Gorge, and the other the Heart.  For what can you, an a woman thus leans upon the purple, and so strews Blandishments that the clear Nature of Facts are either so candied and frosted to a Mystery, or so bemired that they are no find.  Surely it is admirable to have a Fancy and a Fancy when in Love, but why so witless about a witty Insanity ?  It would loom the bigger if stripped of its Jangle, but no, drugged such must go. As foggy as a Mere, as drenched as a Pump ; twittering so loud upon the Wire that one cannot hear the Message. And yet !

# AUGUST *hath 31 days*

---

## DISTEMPERS

WHAT they have in their Heads, Hearts, Stomachs, Pockets, Flaps, Tabs and Plackets, have one and all been some and severally commented on, by way of hint or harsh Harangue, praised, blamed, epicked, poemed and pastoraled, pamphleted, prodded and pushed, made a Spring-board for every sort of Conjecture whatsoever, good, bad and indifferent.

Some have it that they cannot do, have, be, think, act, get, give, go, come, right in anyway. Others that they cannot do, have, be, think, act, get, give, go, wrong in any way, others set them between two Stools saying that they can, yet cannot, that they have and have not, that they think yet think nothing, that they give and yet take, that they are both right and much wrong, that in fact, they swing between two Conditions like a Bell's Clapper, that can never be said to be anywhere, neither in the Centre, nor to the Side, for that which is always moving, is in no settled State long enough to be either damned or transfigured. It is this, perhaps, that has made them too fine for Hell and too swift for Heaven.

Be that as it may, say we, 'tis a gruesome thing when a Woman snaps Grace in twain with a bragging Tongue, for truly such have clack in our City, and run about like mad Dogs, as if Love and its doings were a public Smithy, where all Ears are shod with : "She is so large, so wide, and said she, when we went down to Duty, thus and so, and so she did !" Or as if Love were a Saw-mill whose Dust must be cast in every Eye, or as if it were meet to discuss in public assembly that which by Nature was hidden between two Pillars. The very lowest Ruffian, the most scabby Pimp, or the leanest Wittold would blush and scrape his Shins for Shame of her. Presently then it appears and seems and is in verity, sad chroni-

cling this that all Women are not tidy and neat of Perch,
for when a Woman is sick she is sicker sick than any
Man, as a rotten Plover is more
stincking than a rotten Stick.
Even the Cat scratches to make
Hide of his Intimacies and whis-
pers to the Earth his Secrets, dung-
ing apart not to shame that grave
Necessity which was born in the
Penumbra, and goes to the Shades.

Nay, not so shy are all Women
with their Loves, but doss aloud,
and cackle and crow over the last
to Bed as if she were an Egg and
not a Darling, and run about the
streets after hawking her about,
wriggling and alive, for all to see and piss against! Oh
fie! Oh shame! She fouls everything she touches
with the Droppings natural to her lost Condition!

She is shameless and shameridden! She is haggard
at both Ends, and is the greater shamed that she bleat
of twice one and both the same. And while many a Man
speaks no better, nay often and ever far more naturally
in this Vein, it is but his Nature whining. For that which
is a Mystery, which amazes, terrifies, is sought after and
raised high, that will a Man hound, spring against and
befoul, for very Chagrin. But, doth the Hand tell of the
Palm, the Eye of the Iris, the Tongue of the Mouth? Nay,
'tis a foul Bird that fouls its Finch!

Again, just as there are some Fellows who will brag
that they can teach a Woman much and yet again, and
be her all-in-one, there are, alike, Women, no wiser, who
maintain that they could (had they a Mind to) teach a
taught Woman ; thus though it is sadly against me to
report it of one so curing to the Wound as Patience Scalpel, yet did she (on such Evenings as saw her facing her
favorite Vintage, for no otherwise would she have brought
herself to it,) hint, then aver, and finally boast that she
herself, though all Thumbs at the business and an Ama-
teur, never having gone so much as a Nose-length into
the Matter, could mean as much to a Woman as another,
though the gentle purring of "Nay! Nay! Nay!" from the
Furs surrounding Dame Musset continued to bleed in
her Flank.

"What," said that good Dame, "can you know about
it, who have gentlemaned only ? Recall, and remenber,
my Love, that the Camel is forever facing a Needle, but
cannot go through it, and a Woman is much nearer the
needle's proportion in her probabilities than a Man."

"Still and nevertheless !" said Patience.

At this moment entered the two Doxies, High-Head
and Low-Heel, the opposites that one often meets in this
World of Women.  One (Low-Heel) protesting that women were weak and silly Creatures, but all too dear, the
other (High Head) that they were strong, gallant, twice
as hardy as any Man, and several times his equal in
Brain, but none so precious.

"I hold," said High-Head, "that she is Voltairian

of Breath, that she sheds a sharp Aroma, that her mind is so webbed and threaded with Thought and Fancy that the World sees little of either, for the two are in a Thrall, skull-bound and head-hampered. A man can tell you what he thinks, for it comes spinning, a thin and little Thread, from one and a single Bobbin.

"And I hold," said Low-Heel, "that for just that reason she should not declare herself in possession of her own Opinion, for an Opinion is a single and a nice thing, not two Creatures sitting in Skull, sulking away their Days.

"Yet sometimes," broke in her Companion, "she thinks of new things, my lass, and how do you account for that ?"

"She must come on something, since they untied her Bib and altered the size of her Breech-cloth," said the other, "but what of it ? She is nothing but nice !"

"She is everything but !" cried High-Head. "Is she not the spinning Centre of a spinning World ? Do not the Bees belly and blow, hone their Beaks and hoard their Honey to make her Negus and Nectar ? The Worm, from Head to Heel, one long contriving inch that she may be wrapped in Silks and Satins, the Seal well suppled for her Coat, and the Seed in the Dirt, fattening and bursting for her Delight ? Why, does not Nature, that old Trot, weave Day and Night the Threads of human Destiny whereto these Damsels hold, Chin and Shank, sky-swimming up the Tree that has plotted an hundred Years to coffin her ! Great Mother of Geese, how she crawls !" she added.

ZODIAC

"Nine Pins and ten Pins and Crows to a Cock !" exclaimed her Bride, "How you wander ! such Women as you describe are only seen in Books, or are raked up with the Plough, or are written of in Tomes with the Quill of the Goose that has, with her, been dead a million years, and is Dust with her doings ! And even at that, what have These Scriveners said of her but that she must have had a Testes of sorts, however wried and awander ; that indeed she was called forth a Man, and when answering, by some Mischance, or monstrous Fury of Fate, stumbled over a Womb, and was damned then and forever to drag it about, like a Prisoner his Ball and Chain, whether she would or no."

"Because, sweet Fool," said her Companion, "they cannot let her be, or proclaim her just good Distaff Stuff, but will admit her to sense through the masculine Door only, nevertheless, I've noticed, belabouring her the while they admire, with Remarks to the effect that she be unwieldy, gander-gated, sprung at Hip, unlovely, disenchanting, bearded, hoop-chested, game of Leg, out at Elbow, double-jointed, hook-toothed, splay-footed, wattled, hamstrung, mated with nothing, high-bridged and loose-lipped, no-woman's Meat the length of her Bones, fit for no diddling, dallying Tom, white-eyed and no Wind in her Nostrils but such as blows down her Bellows to make her a neither, and so forth and so on. In no wise worth their pains. For near to a Man or far from a Man, she will not be of him !" She paused "And from where, say you, come such Women ? Up from the

Cellar, down from the Bed of Matrimony, under Sleep and over come. Past watching Eye and seeking Hand and well over Hedge. From Pantry and Bride's-sleep, in Mid-conception and in old Age, from Bank and Culvert, from Bog's Dutch and Fen's marrow, from all walks and all paths, from round Doors and drop Lofts, from Hayricks and Cabbage-patch, from King's Thrones and Clerks' Stools, from high Life and from low. Some dropping Teapots and Linens, some Caddies and Cambric, some Seaweed and Saffron, some with Trophy Skulls and Memory Bones, gleanings from Love's Labour lost. Some in Nightgowns and some in Fashion, some hot with Home work and some cool with Decisions. Indeed, some of all sorts, to swarm in that wide Acre where, beside some brawling March, the first of shes turned up a Hem with the Hand of Combat.

    "Too true for you, perchance", admitted her
        Love. "But nevertheless, did not some
           and several return to their
            Posts ?" "Indeed, and a
             few", said High -
             Head, "but
             *how!*"

★

# SEPTEMBER *hath 30 days*

## HER TIDES AND MOONS

THE very Condition of Woman is so subject to Hazard, so complex, and so grievous, that to place her at one Moment is but to displace her at the next.

In Youth she is comely, straight of Limb, fair of Eye, sweet back and front; tall or short, light or dark--somehow or somewhat to the Heart. Yet it is not twelve span before she sags, stretches, becomes distorted. Her Bones dry, her flesh melts, her Tongue is bitter, or runs an outlawed Honey. Her Mind is corrupt with the Cash of a pick-thank existence. Life has taught her Life. She hath become Friends with it, nor hath she lain long enough upon her Back—though she hath lain so half her duration, to prefer the Coin of Ether. She was not fashioned to swim in Heaven, she is a Fish of Earth, she swims in Terra-firma.

Yet in this poor Condition she causes Pain to Condition as poor. For all are bagged of the same Net, and one comes to as ignoble Ashes as another. The pelvic Bone of Saint Theresa gapes no more Honesty than that of Messalina, for the missing Door wherein no Man passed, is as Not as that windy Space where all were wont to charge, and the Eye that wept for it is as unhoused as the flesh it cried for.

No Feet come and go in the Grave, nor is any Hand wanton in the Tomb, and this is a long while, wherefore then do you grieve? She is dishonest to-day, but to-morrow she is unsought for forever.

Yet we trouble the Heart for that which was made hastily and without peradventure of how it should be in the Womb, and without Wish to know how it shall fare ten weeks in the Earth.

These be three Conditions, yet we take account of

the one and second only, that she is. What then is this but a short swinging of the Mind, a false Addition, for that two Figures of its entirety are left to no accounting?

If then in Man Jealousy for his Wife is an unthinking and amiss Calculation, how much more pointless is it for a Woman to faint, grow sick, turn to Fury and Sorrow over a Woman? A man may rage for the little Difference which shall be alien always, but a Woman tears her Shift for a Likeness in a Shift, and a Mystery that is lost to the proportion of Mystery.

Yet do this Fire rage as hotly here in the Garden of Venus, yea, with an even more licorous and tempestuous flame, than in the very Camp of Nature; and where one Man is cut down from a Rope's End for the sake of his dishonest Wife, two Maids will that same day be found swinging to that Same Beam for that same Girl.

They do not plead, as is the Custom among Families, that they are by Treachery made Cuckold, wear Horns and nourish a bastard Child, for such a contention were more than impossible. And though that has been, for the ancient, the chiefest Thorn in the side, see how vain is Man's suffering, change it how you will, for though that Prick is nowhere in the Flesh of Sister for Sister, they cry as loud, yea, lament still more copiously, turning and twisting as if the very Lack were an extraordinary Pain!

What then is this but a Vanity, and a pouring out of Despair over ourselves; and doth it not prove, all that Man has said to the contrary (bringing the legitimacy of his Offspring to the Bench as reason) that it is a Lie alone, and that the Seat of the Matter is in his own Pride ?

Take away a Man's excuse and he weeps the same, though this time it will be a desolate and unarguing Melancholy. Yet withal 'tis more honest, and the more honest a thing be, the nearer it strikes against the Rib. So it is with Woman. They have no Platform for their Jealousies but the true bitterness of that Folly, and where they weep, it is for Loneliness estranged—the unthinking returning of themselves to themselves, if they but reason—which is improbable : for where there is a Grain of Reason, there is a Grain of recovery, and where there is a Grain of Recovery there is a Blade of Indifference, and where this shoots up, there may be a Garden of Oblivion in which to ease the Breath.

Nevertheless we have become so used to calling Vanity by its other Name, that even a woman wailing for a Woman has not taught us of it. And those who lie down in this Lament turn to the Wall as completely as Penelope lamenting her Husband.

It is a Maze, nor will we have a way out of it, though we know of long that way. Much turning of the Spindle thins out the Thread of Despair, and much leaping of the Shuttle threads Trouble to a Purpose, yet we will none of it, and step the Treadle without Aim, and cast the Shuttle without Food, and weave the air into a Mantle of Sickness.

We shake the Tree, till there be no Leaves, and cry

out at the Sticks ; we trouble the Earth awhile with our
Fury ; our Sorrow is flesh thick, and we shall not cease
to eat of it until the easing Bone. Our Peace is not
skin deep, but to the Marrow, we are not wise this side
of *rigor mortis ;* we go down to no River of Wisdom, but
swim alone in Jordan. We have few Philosophers
among us, for our Blood was stewed too thick
to bear up Wisdom, which is a little
Craft, and floats only when
the way is prepared, and
the Winds are calm.

## LISTS AND LIKELIHOODS

THE Vixen in the Coat of red,
The Hussy with the Honey Head,
Her frontal Bone soft lappéd up
With hempen Ringlets like the Tup,
The Doxy in the Vest of Kid
Rustling like the Katie-did,
With Panther's Eyen dark and wan,
And dovës Feet to walk upon.
The Jockey with the Pelvis plump,
The high-hipped Wrestler with the Rump
Of yearling Mare, firm, sleek and creased,
The Tamer smelling like her Beast,
The starry Jade with mannish Stride,
The Sister Twins in one Sash tied,
The humpback Jester at her ease,
Her Jollies coiled on their Trapeze.
The Virgin with the Patridge Call,
Stepping her rolling azure Ball,
The Queen, who in the Night turned down
The spikës of her Husband's Crown
Therein to sit her Wench of Bliss
The whole long Year will be like this !
For all the Planets, Stars and Zones
Run girlish to their Marrow-bones !
And all the Tides prognosticate
Not much of any other State !

# OCTOBER *hath 31 days*

THERE was a time when still rhymed to the wild Rib that had made her, Woman was atune to every Adder, every Lion, every Tiger, every Wood thing, every Water-wight, every Sky-wanderer; every Apple was to her a whole Superstition, and to quiet and to tame that Bone, she whispered "Lord! Lord!"

But yet a little while and she is most grisly impudent. As the Earth sucked down her Generations, Body for Body, became she less hollow for the Lord's priming. Any prating Fellow with a Lute at bottom, a handful of Frills, a Knee turned out and a sweeping Feather, could, in one Verse, sing her full of Earth, and indeed for what our Minstrels have to account themselves guilty, will perhaps, with the Tibia of Caesar, lie unchartered in the Tomb of no Man's memory a long lethal Æon. He was Lord-my-own and Cock-Sparrow of her trembling, he was both Adder in the Grass and Pippin on the Bough, he was the rush waving and the Bolt upon the Door, and the exceeding crammed Larder wherein she sat filching, a nibbling Mouse of Pang and Pang again.

And yet by yet a Body and a Body went under, and she lost both God and man. So deviled of Appetite that no Food was her winning Portion. God passed, and Man passed and Maternity went by as but the Dust under the Heel of wan marching, and she saw herself becoming thin Batter and no-why's Bread, and she leaned at her Casement and wept most bitterly. She climbed down the Stairs, by Stair made her moan, and into the Streets went by Lamp-post and Pillar, singing and sobbing : "*Auprès de ma blonde!*" by Haberdasher and Butcher. At every Gate and Post she lamented and hummed, her Hands upon the Copings, passing and bewailing, and went yet further and heard the Lark singing, and listened until it was the Heron crying by the Sedges, and the nightfall's true rising nightly nightingale. The Birds were off the

Earth, and the Sky covered with Claws going South, and she sat where the Wheat sprang not and was now a Cud in a Winter Mouth, and she saw that her Years were mounting, and she returned homeward, and Godless and fearless, made Fear and a God of the yellow Hair of Dame Musset, wandering about the grassless Sods of her Garden, leaning aver and anon upon the Sun-dial without its Hours, or bending over the Fountain that never poured forth that gentle Spray for which it and she were pining, or just plain walking, her Hands well wrapped in the Folds of her dust-colored man-saver, or, as it was originally registered and patent applied for, Winter-woolens-for-the-Woman-over-forty.

Did then Daisy Downpour, for so she might as well be called as any other, let down her mouse-colored-insufficient-hemi-spherical-quantity of Hair, thrilled loose a Shoulder, thus exposing to the gaze of Dame Musset (had she looked) the machine-hooked glory of a Pair of near-pink Undergarments, most luringly loosened in the Weave at full good four Points. "If this," said Daisy, "does not secure me God, then a linen Rose tossed at my Love's hour of Need, should bring her to my Surface!"

And casting it, Dame Musset went around and around. Under Foot it went, and down into the Earth, and there descended, Dame Musset still pacing and thinking of a Girl's Eye from which she had skimmed the Milk of Love, and whether she should again promenade the *Impasse des deux Anges*, and trust to the Bed-airing instincts of the said Girl, to bring her in Mob-cap, and all

June of Bosom to the utter third-storey Window left, from which point of Vantage Dame Musset had first

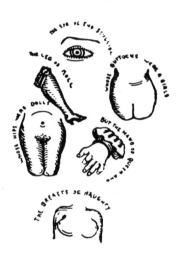

seen her winking a House-wife's Eye at the little Scullion in the Pantry Window opposite, from whom the Bed-airer had remov- ed her Wiles and Ways for a short yet thrifty Glance in the direction of Musset, —or should she not ?  For Flank on Flank, Jew on Christian, had bedded throughout her gentle Fore- fathers to the tune of many an aristocratic Artery athwart many a crude Civilian, to give her the uncertainty now in the Hooves of her Feet, one Heathen and one Gentlewoman, and to make her yet Angle before she stopped to think and to withdraw the Bait from thick Waters and from thin, pleased in the one vein with the Housemaid and in the other sighing for Quality.

Nay, it was beneath her !  As was also the prying, overlooking Eye of Daisy Downpour, for she was known in the *Arrondissement* as Corset maker, and a woman so much of the People that she had clung to them, Palm on Palm, down to the very first, who had decided to plant Orchids in his Bean-rows, and thus started all the strain of difference between a Lady and no Lady at all.

"Alas and alas !" sighed Dame Musset, "to think that

blue Blood should set so many out of reach ! Yet were
I one of the direct Peerage, could I not confer the Order
of the Garter upon her, thus bring her, like a Calf on a
Rope, slowly balking to my Bed, through the Land un-
known, over the hedges of How-So, slipping and sliding
past the Zone of unfit, in by a Leg at least, until incarna-
tion by generation, the Calf becomes the Bird of Paradise,
to lean all moulting Love upon my Spartan Chest, there
to pluck at my heart's Armour, until the Visor is lifted—
but no !" thought she, "I get my Armoury mixed, that
is another Spot !"

Still she paced. "If," said she, "I could mould the
Pot nearer to the Heart's desire, I would have my Scullion's Eye lie in the Head of Billings-On-Coo, with
the Breasts of Haughty on the Hips of Doll, on the
Leg of Moll, with the Shins of Mazie, under the Scullion's Eye which lies in the Head of Billings-On-Coo.
The Buttocks of a Girl I saw take a slip and slither one
peelish day in Fall, when on her way to Devotion in the
side Aisles of the Church of the *St Germain des Prés*, to lie
on the back of the Hips of Doll, on the Leg of Moll, whose
Shins are Mazie's, all under the Eye of the Scullion, Etc.,
and the rowdy Parts of a scampering Jade in Pluckford
Place, on the front of the Back that was a Girl seen one
peelish day, all under the Scullion's Eye, with the Breasts
of Haughty on the Hips of Doll, with the Leg of
Moll, whose Shins are Mazie's, all under the Scullion's
Eye, in the Head of Billings-on-Coo. But the Hand,"
she said, "must be Queen Anne's, to smooth down the Dress

with the rightful and elegant Gesture necessary to cover the Hip that was and the rowdy Part, etc., and the things that there were done ! Oh monstrous Pot !" she sighed, "oh heinous Potter, oh refined, refined, refined Joke, that once smashed to bits it must go a go-going, and when once concocted must eternally be by another's Whim ! We should be able to order our Ladies as we would, and not as they come. Could any haphazard be as choice as I could pick and prefer, if this Dearing were left scattered about at Leg-counter and Head-rack ? Ah, how I could choose were I not floor-walked and pounced upon at every Step !" Yet never by so much as a Feature did she choose, in her roving, one Tendon, nay not so much as a Sternum bone or a coxal of Daisy Downpour ; and by so much Indifference, packed down on Scorn, became she first God, then God Almighty, then God Dumbfounding, and still later God help us, and finally God Damn to Daisy Downpour. Year on Year she leaned in her pink hook-weave Under-kirtel, singing, "*Auprès de ma Blonde*," and Autumn by Autumn tossed a tattered linen Rose, and age by age became more God-haunted and Demon-seeking, until Dame Musset, who was in a way an Amazon unhorsed, feared her more than she noticed her, and noticed her yet more than she liked her, and liked her not at all. "That woman," said she to her Folly, Seño-rita Fly-About, "knows when I go and come, when I bed and when I arise, and all she has asked of me these ten Years is that on the Day I shall find a need of her, I shall place a Pot of Geraniums on my Sill, and she will come flying to me, a Drupe of a Juno in Flannels, to thaw me down, shall I, as I Say but hint that State by the simplest Pot of rosy Geraniums set out upon my Sill, and has turned her Eye that way so long and so tirelessly that I dread me one of these days she will fancy the Flower into growing there indeed, and for such a Catastrophe" she said, sinking into her Furs, and drawing a *duvet* about her, "I shall need Friends, Friends of a noble Tarnish, as flocking as Shad-roe, and all of them stout of Heart, high and sharp of Heel. All Women," she apostrophised, "are not Women all, and I fear that, in yonder Bosom leaning upon her Casement, grows a Garden of Hope, and that with it she would crown and feather me with the Pinions of celestial Glory only to destroy me with these same Implements, for in the Mind," said she, "of the Woman lost twice there is only one Furrow in which to grow a Seed, and much dead Matter to nourish it, and alas ! in that mundane Skull, that Fontanel of Baby-lady-woman, grows one Weed, myself !"

"Be not afraid," twittered Mazie Tuck-and-Frill, "you shall be well surrounded."

"God help us !" said Patience Scalpel, draining her Glass, "not one good hammer-throwing, discus-casting, coxy Prepuce amongst you !"

"Oh wry Luck and wrong cast ! Is the Belly-strap of Venus to slip Sling and slew me to my dimming ? Am I to be cuddled to the Grave in three Pins and a Yard of

warm Woman's Pelt ?" cried Dame Musset. "All in my
willy-nilly years, when I should find Custom only,
and never a sly waylaying Drab in the dark to
gin and make a catch of me, no longing
lingering at Turnstile and Toll-gate,
at Door-lock and Key-hole !"
"Time passes," said Patience.

## SPRING FEVERS, LOVE PHILTERS AND
## WINTER FEASTS

Now, was it the same in the Hap-hour of the World, when whelks whispered in the brink of the Night, rocked in the Cradle of Time's Ditch, taking their Will-of-the-wisp, all in a flux of Tenses and Turns ? The simplicity of their nature was upon them, Cap and Shoe. What they gave out was but the Earth given bide, until some billion of improving Years later, having toiled for the worse, and having made a stink of Advancement, became Queen-Man and King-Woman, under the Bells of the Bride's Wake, and Corpse Sleep, with Butter and Mustard on their Alms-bread for Charity, snitching in Larder cold end upon cold end of most comical Mutton, to fatten the lift to a Strumpet's turn, or buck up her Roup with promise of Glut, bridling her Kick with the trace of Contention ; the Snood upon her a jiffy too late ; greasing the Firkin for the Passover plate—from Slime unto Dream one long Mystery of Æons-pot, steaming on the Hip of the Lamb, bringing us forward, hand over hand, up to the Standard, baa upon bleat, until, we say, we have it presented to us on an Anno Domini Salver, that Christians now think nothing of head-dipping to bite the Pippin in tub-water and Cow's-trough ; while but a thought backward the Heathen, lang syne, heaped Mystic on Magic, to bring about the same end—will she or won't he ?

So Philters and Drams, and which-ways for Maidens all forlorn in tatters of Love's hope.  Drain they not draughts of last Year's Snow, of late year's Bitter, tainted with Sassifras and sickened with Shag, to wax the rough Highway on which Love balks at a canter, to make them a byword of she loves me, he loves me, and the not to the not ?  Some go in Weal Chains and Woe Anchors, neck tied and night worn, Thumb worried and Lip lavished for the good it may cast up on the Knees of the Morrow, or on the Neck of the stiff God of Chance.  But Philter by falter, and Hope upon Clutch, and the more Peels spilt over Shoulder the more spelled of a Girl.  And saying riddle me this, or meddle me that, contriving the Potion as ever you may, hiccup hic jacet, brings up nothing but naught with a Dear on its back.

Was there a whisper of Ellen or Mary, of Rachel or Gretchen, of Tao or Hedda or Bellorinabella y Bellorella, or Tancred of Injen in the Old Winds, or of Wives whispering a thing to a Wife ?  What's in a name before Christ ?  Were all Giants' doings a Man's, and no mountain-top moultings of a Goblin well-papped to the Heel ?  To say nothing and less of Myths Tongue-tied with Girl-talk, or a petal of Dog-fennel seeking a bi-fatal Breeze ?  Blowing inland for Trace, and out-ocean for Scent, and nosing to Ground for Spoor of her want ?  Higg over Bluff, and jogg over Moor, prancing down Gullies and preen up an Alley.  Whirling and hooting of a Miss with her Missus ?  No Time without God, no end without Christ !

In Cave's Mouth it was bruited as Love-by-a-hair,

when the Thigh-bone of Mother brought Daughter to rights, and the Breastbone of wishings, made Weaksisters at home.

We have it clipped from a grass Breeze, and gleaned from a Bluff's brow, Leaf upon Leaf, incredible Autumns deep, forgotten by all but the Blood-hounds of deduction, that Priscilla herself was prone to a Distaff, and garbled her John for her Jenny in Cupboard would get no Dog a Bone.

Winter feast on Summer starve bring all Brooks to churning, and pass the Whey as ever you may, your Hands will print the Butterspot on the Foolscap of confession. So eat your Winter Lettuce, and say your Spring Beads, seek your Mirror, or stand in the cold at the hour of Midnight, or put what you will under your Pillow to know what you can in the Dawn of it, or see the Moon over your Shoulder, roving and hunting the world for an Omen, you'll get her, you'll have her, you'll take her and lose her, you'll miss by an Item, and over-reach by a Yard, undervalue, overestimate, hotbed or cold ! The Branch does not bend unless for a passing, and some must go first, and some must come after. And how is the Jungle so twig-thick and underfoot, if not because a Bison, and a Bison and a Bison went by ?

So take the first Hair from your Head, and boil it with Mare's milk and wrap in a Napkin and bring the Goat inside out, then till the old Mother of six pans of her Earth, and next to the fur-side, lay the Nap to the Horns' end, and thereover cast a peep of No-Doubting-

Sappho, blinked from the Stews of Secret Greek Broth, and some Rennet of Lesbos to force a get-up in the near Resurrection, and put on a Horseshoe to ride Luck's Mare at a Gallop a trot, and when the Mass bubbles and at the River's lip quivers, call it dear Cyprian, and take her under your Wing on the warm side, and but her no buts!

Or would you less Trouble ?

Away Girl !

# NOVEMBER *hath 30 days*

## EBB

CAN one say by what Path, under what Bush, beside what Ditch, beneath what Mountain, through what Manlabour and Slaveswork, Man came upon the Burrows of Wisdom, and sometimes upon the skin of her herself ? No, it cannot be said, for some and most, spend their bright Youth seeking her, while Woman spends her bright Youth brightly avoiding her. And at fifty what has a Man but his wisdom, and what has a Woman, but more suddenly, and therefore more pleasantly, that Wisdom also, for to Man it comes with the stealth of a deep Sleep, and in a Sleep he is when he nods that he has it bagged, but to Woman it comes when she has no cause for Children and no effect for Babes!

Then is she wise!

"What a wind-fall of a moment!" said Dame Musset, when at fifty odd she saw a long stretch of Beach about her. "What a lift in a Cab when there is no Address, what a Staff in Hand when the Hills have come down. Now," she added, "that this tortured old Wineskin can no longer suffer gutting, I shall whirl me about this World indeed, and trifle to the hilt. Yet," mused she, "what is this Safety and Wisdom worth when it comes riding before the Horse? Women must know of it before they can! And damn my Eyes!" said the good dame, "I shall ring the Bells of all Basham for this discovery; and make such a Groaning and tintinabulation throughout my own City, that every Woman will unloosen her Stays and hang them at Window for joy of the thing!"

Therefore she set out through the Town, her Staff in hand, her Busby well over one Eye, and as she went she spoke with Women, indoors and out, and had Words with them on many things that they had not hoped to know for a great long while.

Some wept into Kerchiefs for Love's sake, and yet others swam out into a Dram of Ditchwater, and got their deaths of drowning, or hung Belly up on Halters, and Well-ropes and Kite-strings and near Water-hawsers, and others died in black Gloves, or ate Kickshaw trifles whipped up with Hemlock, from a Pantry that would never creak to their welt again, or yet others drilled, ash by dust and gravel by Hod, earth dipping for a Grave to coverall, or knelt over Mirrors of a bevel asking the world-wise Lie, or all in their Pretties, wept rump up and heart down for the Sorrow and the Pain of Loveslabourlost, while dame Musset sat on a thorn of a Hedgerow (and never the wiser) that she might save a girl or so before she had wallowed in Love's rich welter, or troughed a mouthful at the Tarn of temptation.

"Girl!" she said to the first she saw approaching, "the meat on your Bones cries aloud of Spring in the Fat, yet could I poison you with the Fang of Knowledge, trip you up in your twenties, so that you browse deep on the bog-matter, that is old-girls' Wisdom, would I not do it with a high Heart and gladly, so," said she, "riddle me this : as lame as a Goose, as halt as a Standstill, as fast as a Watch, as wet as a Rill, as soft as a Mouse end, as hard as a Heart, as salt as a flitch, as bitter as Gall, as sweet as the-way-in, as sour as old Cider, as dear as a Darling, as mean as a Boil ; which is always present yet never in Sight, which is as light as a Kerchief, and as dark as a Crow ? That", she said, "is Love, but," added she, "riddle me the other : That is as cool as a Cow's Dug, as sane as a Bellhop, as calm as a Groat, as sure as you-think-it, and as right-as-you-are.   Wisdom.   And which will you have ?"

But the Girl would not listen and said *Gee* to her Oxen.   Then went Dame Musset into Petticoat Lane, just off Breach-String-Alley, where the wash of the World is a dozen of Drawers in the Victorian Style, a Leg for a Leg and a great Gap to span them.   And seeing a Lass coming from Market with little in her Basket to save her from starving but the whole of an Ox with a Tongue out-lolling, a breech-end to the Brisket with a rosette in pucker, and a whole survey of Heaven in the low Light of its Eyes, full fathoms wise in its Eyeballs of dear Eden, a ream and a half of tripe's Meat, that harked back to three Bellies, a fair Pig's Bladder for Baby to call the Cattle home, and a round of Hares' Fur to make Daddy a coat, with a Nose-bag of Carrots and a jugfull of rye, and a Mill on her back to winnow the apples in her Winter Acre into kegs of Home-brewing for a Guest and a Secret the whole Winter through,—to this one said Musset, as the Geese flocked ungainly, "Hold Wench, there is much you must learn ere you cram that Fodder down the Gorge of your Gut, and it is of Love and its Sorrow, which, with my new findings, may be turned into a matter of no Tears nor Agues, so but listen and give yea, while I make you, for no-gold, as wise as your Mother, so riddle me this —"

But the Lass would not listen, and said *cluck* to her Geese, and Dame Musset went further into Highhip Road, and there on the steps of the Palace saw Girls of all sorts, in their lute strings and Velvets, their Rag-tags of Sodom and their flaps of Gomorrah and all of them hiding a Letter between them, and none of them twenty, and all had the Hound's Eye and the Heart dumbfounded, and the stagger of those penned in the Pastures of Hope, far on the way to the Shambles of Know-all-and-try-all, and Dame Musset became exceeding sorry, though no Vein bled, for Knowledge has cooled from Perron to Chimney.

"Girls, Girls," said she, "pause now to listen, I bring no Trumpet but that of my Message. I ask you to settle on the Borders of yonder Palace, like Doves on a Fort, nor lift to fly until you have had word with me, for I have come to deliver you from Love and Love's Folly, and great Regrets that furl up like Thunder, and in terrible Banners outrun to bedamn you. So riddle me this—"

But the Girls would not listen, and lifted their Skirts making a swish going outward, and Dame Musset went still further into Brambelly Grove, where Women are Women, and all of them busy in whipping the Sorrow from the Potluck of the other, like Linens they lay, over

Box hedge and Rose-bush, all a cry stained sprawling.

"Yet hold !" cried Dame Musset, "though this is a rare Sight and one that I would not have missed for Shank or my Shin, still I've seen it, and 'tis sufficient, so rise up and Arm down, I come to give you Word that will make of this business a silly trouncing and no thing for Tears, so riddle me this —"

But they would not listen, and the Whip fell and the Girls wept, all in the Hedges of Brambelly Grove.

So Dame Musset went further until she came to Wellover Square, where she saw a Madame in Mittens sipping her Tea by the Gates of the Ministry. She came to a stop, and as if she had been a Crier of old London she had her say in this manner :

"Madam, I shall waste none of your Time by asking for it. This Morning, just as the Clock struck three of the Dawn, I came down from the strident winds of Life's Troubles, a flag in no breeze, and I saw how and in what manner I might save the world all its Trials and Troubles, even for such as are silly enough to be in Love with a Man and a Man. This Wisdom came like a Sheep from the fold, and the Hound of Torment leapt for a Newbride's Bosom. It has thus been my Pleasure, as it has been that of all over fifty, to know wherein I have erred. Now, had I this Knowledge when I was ten and ten and not yet ten, I should have had yet greater nights, and no tears wasting and reeking my Linens, so I give it to you : Never want but what you have, never have but that which stays, and let nothing remain. Wisdom is indifference, the only

Trouble with it," said she, pausing, "is how extraordinarily it fills the Bed. For this Morning, not half an Hour after my Wisdom had come down upon me, ten Girls I had tried vainly for but a Month gone, were all tearing at my shutters —"

"Ah yes," said the Madame, putting another Lump in her tea, "I am sixty, and at my Age both Youth and Wisdom are over, and you reap a third Crop."

"God save us," cried Dame Musset, "is there yet more to learn of this world ?"

"But yes," said the Crone, "there is that and others. At sixty you are ten Years tired of your Knowledge."

Then returned Dame Musset by the way she had come, and *en route* remanded her order for ringing of Bells.

# DECEMBER *hath 31 days*

I N this cold and chill December, the Month of the
Year when the proof of God died, died Saint Musset,
proof of Earth, for she had loosened and come up-
rooted in the Path of Love, where she had so long flour-
ished. Nor yet with any alien Sickness came she to
her Death, but as one who had a grave Commission
and the ambassador recalled.

She had blossomed on Sap's need, and when need's Sap found such easy flowing in the Year of our Lord 19— what more was there for her to do ? Yet though her Life was completed, she has many Transactions for her end, so said she, lying on the flat of her Back, her good Beak of a nose yet more of a Pope's proportion, "I have heard somewhere that there be as many Burials, and as different, as there be Births, yea, even in excess of this, for a Babe is born one of two ways, Head or Foot, but a Corpse can go down all-in-one or bit by bit, sideways or lengthways or Shin to Chin.  There is the Small-town Burial and the Burial of State, and the Burial of Harvest, and the Burial of Frost.  There is cracking and crating as they understand it in the District of the Ganges, and there is the upright and the supine, and the Head to Heel, there is Urn Burial or Cremation, there is the Flesh-eating Stone, the Sarcophagus, there is embalming and stretching of the Gut, there is lamenting, and there is laughing, There are those buried in Trenches, and those in Tombs, and those on Hills and those in Dales, those buried of shallow and those of deep digging. Some are followed on Foot, and some are followed in Carriages, and some are followed in the Mind alone and some are not followed at all ; some have a Christian and some a Pagan rite, and some are swallowed up for an Hour in Churches, and others are accompanied with Wine and Song and covered with the Leaves of the Day, the while the Ass brays in the Market-place, and the sound of the Wine-press is like the Gush of a Girl's first Sorrow.

"Now I leave behind me, to those who shall follow, or I much mistake my Prowess in these ripe Days of my Life (she having reached a good ninety-nine), many Mourners of many Races and many Tempers, and as they loved me differently in Life so I would have them plan differently for me in Death. Think then of as many manner of Rites of Interment and ending, burning and cracking as there be ingenuity, only", she said in that logical Measure that had made her a great Politician all the days of her Hour, "plan differently, for if you burn me first, how shall you lay me out for shriving, and how, if you drop me in Ocean, can you also bind me with Earth ? Nay, you must come to the matter with Forethought and no Jealousies, so that I stay not too long in that condition, which left to Nature, is most unseemly, like many of her raw Tricks. Therefore provide a Council, and plan with Fecundity, and bring about as good a Series as the Wits of Women can devise."

So it was that when she came to die, there were many so hard pressed with lamenting, and some so glut with Vanity, and others so spoiled of Thought, that a wrangling was heard for full forty-eight Hours, the while she lay easily, as if she sensed in them a little old time Custom.

First forty Women shaved their Heads (all but Señorita Fly-About who for no Woman, quick or dead, would alter her Charm) and carried her through the City on a monstrous Catafalque, and then in forty different Heights these Women went down upon their knees in the darkness of the Catholic Church, and then she was sealed in a Tomb for many days, and the Women twittered about the Tomb like Birds about the Border of a Storm : and then they bore her to the Crossroads, and at every Crossway the Bier was laid down. And a Bird came, and in passing, crowed lamentably, though but that instant an Oat had descended into the dark of its Craw, and a little later at another Crossroad a Hare came, and standing upon the Lid, beat thrice with its custom of hind-foot Mating, and yet further on, a Mountain Goat that way going, threw its Beard up, and lamented bitterly from between its even row of Teeth that knew only the Grass going inward and no word over, and a little later, (there were many Forks going hither and thither, for the Spring in the Grass had seen many herds going four ways, and Love making a common pasture for a Season, what with moo and bray and Hoof and Heel stamping for tell tale), a Night-owl came and sat upon one end of the great and ebon Tassels, and said, or so the Parishioners aver, "Oh ! God !" as if it were his Heart's first Need, and still later a Ground thing, not to this day identified, came upward out of the Earth, and stood awhile, and still purblind and lidless, shook its Fur from Throat to Tail in one long, slow Undulation of Misery, and descended again. Now, a Tup, so new with Life that it walked on Waves came and raising its God's Gift of a Mouth, said "Baaaaa !" And so it was that they hurried on and laid her in the Earth of a little Village, and then they put her low in a great City, and some buried her shallow and some deep, and Women who had not told their Husbands every-

thing, joined them.   And there was veiled Face downcast, and bare Face upturned, and some lamenting sideways and some forward, and some who struck their Hands together, and some who carried them one on one.   And they carved her many Tombs, and many sayings, and much Poetry was cast for her, and in the end they put her upon a great Pyre and burned her to the Heart, warming her Urn for her with their Hands, as a good Wine-bibber warms his Cup of Wine.   And when they came to the ash that was left of her, all had burned but the Tongue, and this flamed, and would not suffer Ash, and it played about upon the handful that had been she indeed.   And seeing this, there was a great Commotion, and the sound of Skirts swirled in haste, and the Patter of much running in feet, but Señorita Fly-About came down upon that Urn first, and beatitude played and flickered upon her Face, and from under her Skirts a slow Smoke issued, though no thing burned, and the Mourners barked about her covetously, and all Night through, it was bruited abroad that the barking continued, like the mournful baying of Hounds in the Hills, though by Dawn there was no sound, And as the day came some hundred Women were seen bent in Prayer.   And yet a little later between them in its Urn on high, they took the Ashes and the Fire, and placed it on the Altar in the Temple of Love.   There it is said, it flickers to this day, and one may still decipher the Line,
beneath its Handles, "Oh ye
of little Faith."

HERE I BE
SAY ALAS!
FOR A PRESENT
BUT FOR MASS
STRUT A PHEASANT
SALT TO LEAVEN
CANDLES SEVEN
WHEN IVE RISEN
SAY THE PRAYER
WHERE MOUNT I
BE NO STAIR
BE NO ROPE
BE NO RUNG
MY WAY HUNG

## MASS

# AFTERWORD

*L*adies *Almanack* was written in early 1928 as a diver-
sion (Barnes later told her friend Hank O'Neal) while
tending her hospitalized lover Thelma Wood. It has
long been assumed to be no more than an affectionate
lampoon of the expatriate lesbian circle to which they
belonged in Paris, and which gathered at the salon of Natalie

Clifford Barney, a Cincinnati heiress. Barnes did not
originally intend to publish the manuscript, she claimed,
but arrangements were soon made to bring the book out
with Edward Titus's Black Manikin Press. In his *Published
in Paris*, Hugh Ford reports: "Plans to issue it under his
auspices ended, though, when the publisher, after agreeing
to defray all costs in return for permission to retain a few
copies which he would put on sale at his shop, provoked
Miss Barnes by asking for money and then demanding
wholesale and retail rights over the book with no assurance
of distribution. The impasse was resolved, at least partly, by
Robert McAlmon, who paid for the printing as a gift to the
author." An edition of 1,050 copies was printed in Dijon
at the Darantière Press (Maurice Darantière had printed
*Ulysses* six years earlier), the first fifty copies hand-colored
by Barnes herself with the assistance of Tylia Perlmutter.
Lacking a standard distributor, the book was "merrily and
effectively hawked along the Left Bank by bold young
women," as Andrew Field writes in his biography of Barnes.

Natalie Barney figures as Evangeline Musset, whose
biography the *Almanack* purports to be, and who was
delighted by the tale. (She too apparently helped with
publication costs.) Andrew Field identifies the rest of the
book's dramatis personae:

> I was shown Natalie Barney's own copy of the book in which
> she has neatly marked all the characters in the margins for
> history. Patience Scalpel, who alternates with the narrator
> of the tale, is Mina Loy [whom Field later describes as
> "the token heterosexual among the Barney women"].

Señorita Fly-About, One of Buzzing Much to Rome, is
Mimi Franchetti, the black-sheep daughter of a noble Italian
family, and she is linked with Doll Furious, actually Dorothy
or Dolly Wilde, who also called herself Oscaria and was
Wilde's niece. (She also had a remarkable facial similarity
to Wilde.) The two British Women of the month of March,
Lady Buck-and-Balk, with a monocle, and Lady Tilly-
Tweed-in-Blood, with a Stetson, are Lady Una Trowbridge
and Radclyffe Hall. They believe in marriage but only of
women to women and would do away with Man altogether.
Bounding Bess, the woman hunted by Dame Musset and the
members of her Sect in order that she be "well branded, i'
the Bottom, Flank, or Buttocks-boss," is Esther Murphy,
who was a great champion of the superiority of women and
would on occasion stride about with a rather large whip.
Cynic Sal—"she dressed like a Coachman of the period
of Pecksniff"—Dame Musset's final choice in love, is
Romaine Brooks, who wore a man's top hat. Among the
flitting characters are Natalie's sister Laura, who is Sister,
and "one dear old Countess," who is Ilse Baroness
Deslandes, an old lover with whom Natalie had regular
fiery quarrels. The page figures who bob about in the text
are Janet Flanner and Solita Solano, who lived together for
several decades. Of all the ladies who figure in *Ladies
Almanack* only Janet Flanner publicly pointed to her
presence in the book, with considerable pleasure, years
later in her *Paris Was Yesterday*.

The illustrations, similar to those in Barnes's novel
*Ryder* (published earlier that year), were modeled after
old picture books she picked up at Paris bookstalls. The

language likewise is derived from older models: Chaucer, the King James Bible, Robert Burton's *Anatomy of Melancholy*—one of her favorite books and especially prominent in the chapter on April (pp. 27-29)—and any number of Restoration dramatists. But the language is also contemporary with some of the experiments Joyce was making: the American poet Jack Hirschman has noted verbal similarities between lines in *Ladies Almanack* and Joyce's *Finnegans Wake*, parts of which Joyce read aloud to Barnes in the twenties (and which she no doubt was reading in installments in *transition*). Barnes's language also anticipates that of several more recent stylists: Edward Dahlberg, who met Barnes in Paris in the twenties, later adopted an archaic style close to the one Barnes used in *Ryder* and *Ladies Almanack*, and similar pastiches of older styles can be found in the fiction of John Barth (*The Sot-Weed Factor*), Gilbert Sorrentino (parts of *Mulligan Stew* and especially *Blue Pastoral*), Erica Jong (*Fanny*), Emma Tennant (*The Adventures of Robina*), and in the writings of Alexander Theroux.

To the end of her life Barnes dismissed *Ladies Almanack* as a trifle, hardly to be taken seriously. She allowed Fran McCullough of Harper & Row to bring out an authorized reprint largely to forestall any unauthorized editions. (Barnes had failed to register the original for copyright.) But her indifference "may have been a pose on Barnes's part," O'Neal speculates; "when it was reissued by Harper & Row in 1972 she wrote an appropriately convoluted foreword and at some point considered revising portions of it. I saw at least one new manuscript page among her papers with the heading 'new page for *Ladies Almanack.*' "

In recent years, feminist critics have suggested that *Ladies Almanack* is considerably more than "an affectionate lampoon," as I referred to it in my first paragraph. It may be more bitter than affectionate (Karla Jay) or a celebration of lesbianism rather than a lampoon (Susan Sniader Lanser). (For a sampling of recent criticism, see the essays on *Ladies Almanack* by Jay, Lanser, and others in Mary Lynn Broe's splendid anthology *Silence and Power* as well as the chapter on Barnes in Shari Benstock's *Women of the Left Bank.*) This new edition should broaden the audience for this subversive little classic.

STEVEN MOORE

WORKS CITED

Benstock, Shari. *Women of the Left Bank: Paris, 1900-1940.* Austin: University of Texas Press, 1986.

Broe, Mary Lynn, ed. *Silence and Power: A Reevaluation of Djuna Barnes.* Carbondale: Southern Illinois University Press, 1991.

Field, Andrew. *Djuna: The Life and Times of Djuna Barnes.* New York: Putnam, 1983.

Ford, Hugh. *Published in Paris: A Literary Chronicle of Paris in the 1920s and 1930s.* New York: Macmillan, 1975.

Hirschman, Jack Aaron. "The Orchestrated Novel: A Study of Poetic Devices in Novels of Djuna Barnes and Hermann Broch, and the Influence of the Works of James Joyce upon Them." Ph.D. diss. Indiana University, 1962.

O'Neal, Hank. *"Life is painful, nasty and short . . . in my case it has only been painful and nasty": Djuna Barnes 1978-1981.* New York: Paragon, 1990.

# DALKEY ARCHIVE PAPERBACKS

## FICTION: AMERICAN

# DALKEY ARCHIVE PAPERBACKS

## FICTION: BRITISH

| | |
|---|---|
| BROOKE-ROSE, CHRISTINE. *Amalgamemnon* | 9.95 |
| CHARTERIS, HUGO. *The Tide Is Right* | 9.95 |
| FIRBANK, RONALD. *Complete Short Stories* | 9.95 |
| MOSLEY, NICHOLAS. *Accident* | 9.95 |
| MOSLEY, NICHOLAS. *Impossible Object* | 9.95 |
| MOSLEY, NICHOLAS. *Judith* | 10.95 |

## FICTION: FRENCH

| | |
|---|---|
| CREVEL, RENÉ. *Putting My Foot in It* | 9.95 |
| ERNAUX, ANNIE. *Cleaned Out* | 9.95 |
| GRAINVILLE, PATRICK. *The Cave of Heaven* | 10.95 |
| NAVARRE, YVES. *Our Share of Time* | 9.95 |
| QUENEAU, RAYMOND. *The Last Days* | 9.95 |
| QUENEAU, RAYMOND. *Pierrot Mon Ami* | 9.95 |
| ROUBAUD, JACQUES. *The Great Fire of London* | 12.95 |
| ROUBAUD, JACQUES. *The Princess Hoppy* | 9.95 |
| SIMON, CLAUDE. *The Invitation* | 9.95 |

## FICTION: IRISH

| | |
|---|---|
| CUSACK, RALPH. *Cadenza* | 7.95 |
| MACLOCHLAINN, ALF. *Out of Focus* | 5.95 |
| O'BRIEN, FLANN. *The Dalkey Archive* | 9.95 |
| O'BRIEN, FLANN. *The Hard Life* | 9.95 |

## FICTION: LATIN AMERICAN and SPANISH

| | |
|---|---|
| CAMPOS, JULIETA. *The Fear of Losing Eurydice* | 8.95 |
| SARDUY, SEVERO. *Cobra* and *Maitreya* | 13.95 |
| TUSQUETS, ESTHER. *Stranded* | 9.95 |
| VALENZUELA, LUISA. *He Who Searches* | 8.00 |

# DALKEY ARCHIVE PAPERBACKS

## POETRY

## NONFICTION

For a complete catalog of our titles, or to order any of these books, write to Dalkey Archive Press, Illinois State University, Campus Box 4241, Normal, IL 61790-4241. One book, 10% off; two books or more, 20% off; add $3.00 postage and handling. Phone orders: (309) 438-7555.